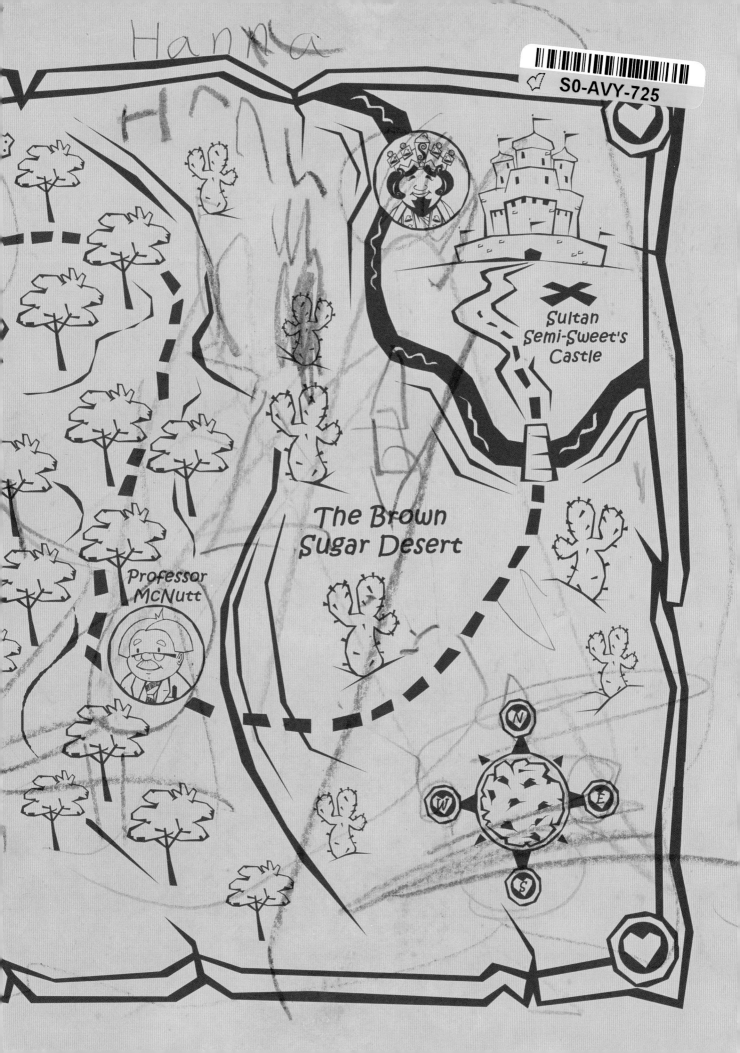

No More Chocolate Chips

Created by Christine Harris-Amos

Written by Dr. Lindamichellebaron

Illustrated by Leslie Harrington

SOMA, LLC

♥ For my mom, Ruth, who taught me how to bake chocolate chip cookies with love ♥ –CHA

To my mother, Dorothy Baron, who never baked me cookies. She did make me a chip off the old chocolate block. –LMB

Especially for Mom, Dad and Mike, all my friends who know the story, and my "armchair buddies", Haggis and Hamish. –LH

Soma, LLC
P.O. Box 897
Kailua, Hawaii 96734
808-261-6075

www.chipandcookie.com

ISBN: 0-9759034-0-3

Library of Congress Cataloging-in-Publication Data
Available upon request

Editor: Michelle R. McCann
Interior Design: Barbara Leese
Cover Design: Leslie Harrington
Printed in Hong Kong

Chip & Cookie's Destiny

Chip & Cookie are "Ambassadors of Reading" encouraging children to read and learn together. They believe that books help create a solid foundation for a successful and enjoyable life. Reading takes you everywhere!

Far, far away, in the tiny village of Raspberry Swirl lived Aunt Della in her cozy white cottage.

Early every morning the children of the village helped Aunt Della bake her delicious chocolate chip cookies. Together they stirred the chocolaty chips and crunchy pecans into the buttery dough. Then they baked the cookies until they were perfectly golden brown.

As they munched the still-warm-from-the-oven cookies, they laughed and told stories and played games. During these baking parties, everyone felt warm inside, even after they ate the very last cookie.

One afternoon Aunt Della sat in her rocking chair looking sadly at her cookie recipe. She had just enough chocolate chips left to make one tiny batch. Sultan Semi-Sweet, the Keeper of All Chocolate, had stopped sending chips and Aunt Della couldn't bake cookies without them.

The children were coming the next morning and she didn't know what to do. Aunt Della thought and thought and thought some more.

Finally, she had an idea!

From her sewing basket she pulled out light and dark brown fabric. She cut the light fabric into two big circles and the dark fabric into lots of tiny circles, then she sewed the tiny circles onto the bigger circles. Finally, she stitched on arms, legs and smiling faces.

When she was finished, Aunt Della gave her dolls a big hug. Magically, as if they were baking, the dolls plumped up and up until their toes danced inside their shoes and their eyes twinkled with laughter.

"Hi Aunt Della.
I'm Chip," shouted
the boy cookie
as he jumped to
his feet.

"And you can call me
Cookie," said the girl
cookie with a grin.

The next morning the children played with Chip and Cookie. They had so much fun they forgot all about their baking party. But Aunt Della didn't forget: still no chocolate chips from Sultan Semi-Sweet!

"Where does the Sultan live?" Chip asked.

"His Chocolate Castle is all the way on the other side of the Brown Sugar Desert."

"We'll go talk to him!" Chip shouted.

"Yes. We'll ask him to send more chips," said Cookie.

"Oh, thank you," said Aunt Della, and she tucked a map into Cookie's backpack.

As Chip and Cookie got ready to leave, Aunt Della baked her last batch of cookies. There were only enough chips to make three, and when she pulled them out of the oven, they were shaped like hearts.

"These must be magic cookies," she told them. "They look like hearts because they are from my heart. Their magic is love."

She tucked the hearts into Chip's backpack and hugged her friends good-bye.

As they walked down the path and out of Raspberry Swirl, Chip and Cookie made up a song to help them remember Aunt Della's words:

Cookies are love you have to share.
Take cookies and love everywhere.
The more you give the better you feel.
Their magic is love and that's for real!

Chip and Cookie started their adventure by crossing Vanilla Pond on the Peppermint Stick Ferry. As they stepped off the boat, they saw Sally, one of the children from the village, moping in Buttercup Meadow.

"What are you doing here?" they asked.

"I was looking for chocolate chips for Aunt Della's baking party," she sighed. "But now I'm lost."

"We're going to find Sultan Semi-Sweet to ask him to send more chips," said Cookie. "Why don't you wait for us here and we'll go back to Raspberry Swirl together?"

"You can collect butter from Buttercup Meadow and vanilla from Vanilla Pond for the cookies," said Chip.

"I better get started," said Sally, smiling because she had such an important job to do.

And just to make sure Sally felt better, Chip gave her a heart-shaped cookie. Then he and Cookie sang:

Cookies are love you have to share.
Take cookies and love everywhere.
The more you give the better you feel.
Their magic is love and that's for real!

Chip and Cookie walked into a grove of trees, where they bumped into a man carrying a tree and a shovel.

"Excuse me," said Chip.

"Oh, thank you!" said the stranger. "I'm Professor McNutt and I'm so glad you bumped into me. I'm lonely here with no one to talk to."

"If you're lonely, why do you stay?" asked Cookie.

"I take care of these trees that grow perfect pecans," he said. "Why don't you stay with me? You can eat pecans all day long."

"We can't stay," said Chip "But we'll meet you on our way back."

Professor McNutt still looked sad, so Chip gave him a heart-shaped cookie. Then he and Cookie sang:

Cookies are love you have to share.
Take cookies and love everywhere.
The more you give the better you feel.
Their magic is love and that's for real!

Professor McNutt smiled. "See you soon!" he shouted as Chip and Cookie continued on their way.

Next they came to the Brown Sugar Desert. Golden dunes stretched as far as their eyes could see.

"The Sultan's castle is still so far away," sighed Cookie. "I'm tired."

"Me too," said Chip. "And my feet hurt."

They both wanted to turn around and go home. Then Cookie remembered how much the children of Raspberry Swirl loved their baking parties.

"Aunt Della and the children are counting on us," she said. "We can't give up now!"

"Let's go find the Sultan!" Chip agreed.

They trudged for hours across the dunes, until finally they saw the Sultan's castle on the horizon: milk chocolate walls, dark chocolate domes and white chocolate towers.

They were almost there!

Chip and Cookie hurried across the bridge and knocked on the castle door.

BOOM! BOOM! BOOM!

When no one answered they pushed open the door and went inside. It was so dark in the castle that they couldn't see a thing, but they could hear strange rumbling and grumbling sounds above them.

Chip and Cookie ran upstairs to investigate.

Behind the two giant chocolate doors at the top of the stairway, the rumbling and grumbling grew louder. Chip and Cookie tiptoed inside, where they found Sultan Semi-Sweet rumbling and grumbling in his sleep.

"Excuse us, please, Mr.... uh... Sultan Semi-Sweet?"
The Sultan didn't answer. He just rumbled and grumbled some more.

"Maybe he can't hear us," said Chip.
They spoke a little louder this time, "Excuse us, pretty please, uh... Mr.... uh.... Sultan Semi-Sweet?"

This time the Sultan's eyes popped open and he roared, "Who are you!"

"I'm... I mean we... uh, I'm Chip."

"And I'm... I'm Cookie."

"What are you doing here?" the Sultan roared again.

Chip was so scared his words flew out, "We came from Raspberry Swirl and Aunt Della can't make cookies because she's out of chocolate chips and the children can't have their baking parties."

"Won't you please send more chips?" Cookie finished.

The Sultan roared even louder, "I will NEVER, EVER send more chocolate chips to Aunt Della!"

Chip and Cookie were shaking in their shoes. They wanted to race out the door, but then the Sultan's roar turned into sobs.

"What's wrong?" they asked.

"What's wrong? What's wrong? Aunt Della and those children always want my chocolate chips for their silly old baking party, but nobody ever invites me!"

The Sultan was so sad Chip and Cookie felt like crying, too. "Maybe this will make you feel better," said Chip, handing the Sultan a heart-shaped cookie. He and Cookie sang:

Cookies are love you have to share.
Take cookies and love everywhere.
The more you give the better you feel.
Their magic is love and that's for real!

Sultan Semi-Sweet stopped crying, and slowly a smile bloomed on his face. "Thank you. I do feel better."

"I have an idea!" said Chip, whispering in the Sultan's ear.

The Sultan whistled for his flying chariot. Chip and Cookie petted the prancing chocolate horses, then loaded the chariot with baskets of chocolate chips. In no time, they were off to finish their adventure.

Once again, Aunt Della was sadly rocking in her chair. This time she was worried about Chip and Cookie. They had been gone so long. Would they ever return?

Suddenly, Aunt Della heard voices singing. It was Chip and Cookie! They were home! She was so happy she hugged herself.

When Aunt Della opened the door, she could hardly believe her eyes. There were her homemade cookie dolls leading a parade of people up the path toward her cottage.

Sally carried the butter and vanilla. Professor McNutt clutched a small pecan tree and was grinning from ear to ear. And wonder of wonders, there was Sultan Semi-Sweet, loaded with baskets and baskets of chocolate chips.

Aunt Della hugged each of them and then rushed back inside to mix up the biggest batch of cookie dough ever.

Once again, Aunt Della's baking party was filled with laughter, games, stories and the smell of fresh baked cookies. But most of all it was filled with love.

Professor McNutt planted his little tree right there in Aunt Della's garden so she would always have perfect pecans for her cookies. And at the end of the party, the village children made a circle around Sultan Semi-Sweet and sang the cookie song in his honor:

> Cookies are love you have to share.
> Take cookies and love everywhere.
> The more you give the better you feel.
> Their magic is love and that's for real!

They all shared their love—and their chocolate chip cookies—forever after.

Aunt Della's Chocolate Chip Cookie Recipe

Preheat oven to 375 degrees for gas oven or 350 degrees for electric.

Blend together until creamy:
2 sticks (1 cup) soft butter from Buttercup Meadow
3/4 cup brown sugar from Brown Sugar Desert
3/4 cup white sugar
2 eggs
1 tsp. Watkins Vanilla from Vanilla Pond

Stir in:
2 1/4 cups all purpose flour
1 level tsp. baking soda
1/2 tsp. salt

Add:
2 cups of the Sultan's semi-sweet chocolate chips
3/4 cup of Professor McNutt's pecan pieces

Don't forget to mix in a healthy portion of love!

Drop the batter from a teaspoon onto a cookie sheet, leaving lots of room in between each cookie. Bake with love for about 12 minutes, or until the cookies are as brown as you wish. Serve with milk or juice and share with friends.